The Tree That Grew To The Moon

Eugenie Fernandes

Scholastic Canada Ltd.

Scholastic Canada Ltd.
123 Newkirk Road, Richmond Hill, Ontario, Canada L4C 3G5

Scholastic Inc.
555 Broadway, New York, NY 10012, USA

Scholastic New Zealand Limited
Private Bag 94407, Greenmount, Auckland, New Zealand

Scholastic Australia Pty Limited
PO Box 579, Gosford, NSW 2250, Australia

Scholastic Ltd.
Villiers House, Clarendon Avenue, Leamington Spa
Warwickshire CV32 5PR, UK

*The illustrations for this book were done in gouache and oil
pastel, with some water colour pencil. A razor blade was used
for scratching.*

Canadian Cataloguing in Publication Data

Fernandes, Eugenie, 1943-
The tree that grew to the moon

ISBN 0-590-24126-5 (bound) — ISBN 0-590-24936-3 (pbk.)

I. Title.

PS8561.E75T7   1994   jC813'.54   C93-094397-X
PZ7.F47Tr 1994

5 4 3 2 1   Printed in Canada   6 7 8 9/9

For my mother
who grew up in Brooklyn
and taught me to love trees.

It was a sizzling summer day.
Lena did *not* want to play outside anymore.
"Too hot," she said. "I'm going home."
On the way she found a baby tree,
uprooted and limp, lying on the sidewalk.

"Aw," said Lena. "Poor thing!"
Carefully she picked it up and hurried home.

Lena took the tree into
the shower to cool it off.
The baby tree liked
the shower.
Then Lena planted the
baby tree in a bag of dirt
in the middle of her room.

"Maybe you shouldn't
plant it there," said Mother.

"Why not?" said Lena.
"What could happen?"

4

"What could happen?" said Mother.
"I'll tell you what could happen.

The roots could wiggle down
into Mr. Podd's apartment
and get all tangled up with his stuff."

"And the branches could wiggle up into your room," said Mother.

Lena smiled. "It will be a jungle in here."

"Exactly," said Mother. "How will I find you then?"

"You won't," said Lena. "*I* will find *you*."

"Maybe I'll put up a swing," said Lena, "and go zooming up to the ceiling and leaping off onto my bed."

"That would make a terrible racket," said Mother. "When Auntie Grump comes for a visit she will say, 'What *is* that horrible noise? Really, dear, you have such uproarious neighbours!' Then she will leave without finishing her tea."

"I will leap quietly," whispered Lena.

"I certainly hope so," said Mother.

"I might build a tree house
in my bedroom," said Lena,

"with bridges and trap doors,
and pulleys for hauling up food."

13

"All of my friends
will come over to play,
and they'll probably
stay for a month —
maybe two!"

Mother shook her head.
"Imagine the chaos,"
she said.

"Pretty soon the branches will grow
out the window," said Lena.
"Then all sorts of wild creatures
will come to live in my tree."

"Good grief!" said Mother.

"Don't worry," said Lena.
"I'll take good care of the creatures.
You won't even know they're here."

"Your tree might grow and grow," said Mother,
"till it crunches right through the ceiling
and into Ms Deertoes' apartment upstairs.
Then what if it keeps on growing?
What if it carries Ms Deertoes
all the way up to the moon?"

"She might like that," said Lena.
"Maybe she'll marry the Man in the Moon
and live happily ever after."

"Perhaps. . . . " sighed Mother. "But of course,
we will still have a gigantic hole in the roof."

"In the winter there will be snowdrifts
in the bedroom," said Mother.

20

"Excellent!" cried Lena.
"I will build an igloo over my bed."

"Eventually,"
said Mother,
"the police will
gallop in here
on their horses
and say it's against
the building code
to have a tree
growing out
of the roof.
What then?"

"Hmm," said Lena.
"*Then* I will plant
my tree outside in
that space in the
sidewalk."

"It will be nice and
cool underneath my
tree, and we will play
in the shade.
The air will be clean.
The old people will
laugh, and the babies
will stop crying.
My tree will be covered
with beautiful flowers,
and all kinds of fruit
for us to eat."

"The mayor will be so happy
he'll have a party for the whole city
right here on our street. There will be
music and dancing and acrobats
and clowns and costumes and a parade.

Ms Deertoes will come back down
with the Man in the Moon,
and maybe some Martians, too.
It will be fantastic!
Everybody will love my tree."

Mother thought about it
for a moment.
Finally she said,
"I think you're right."

After that, Mother and Lena
took very good care
of the baby tree.
They watered it
and fed it.
They read it stories
and played music
to help it grow.

"Do you think it will grow
to the moon?" said Lena.

"You never know," said Mother.
"We'll just have to wait and see."